Treasured Tales

Edited By Donna Samworth

First published in Great Britain in 2023 by:

Young Writers
Remus House
Coltsfoot Drive
Peterborough
PE2 9BF
Telephone: 01733 890066
Website: www.youngwriters.co.uk

Printed and bound in the UK by BookPrintingUK
Website: www.bookprintinguk.com
YB0560Q

Welcome!

Dear Reader,

Welcome to a world of imagination!

My First Story was designed for 5-7 year-olds as an introduction to creative writing and to promote an enjoyment of reading and writing from an early age.

The simple, fun storyboards give even the youngest and most reluctant writers the chance to become interested in literacy by giving them a framework within which to shape their ideas. Pupils could also choose to write without the storyboards, allowing older children to let their creativity flow as much as possible, encouraging the use of imagination and descriptive language.

We believe that seeing their work in print will inspire a love of reading and writing and give these young writers the confidence to develop their skills in the future.

There is nothing like the imagination of children, and this is reflected in the creativity and individuality of the stories in this anthology. I hope you'll enjoy reading their first stories as much as we have.

Imagine. .

Each child was given the beginning of a story and then chose one of five storyboards, using the pictures and their imagination to complete the tale. You can view the storyboards at the end of this book.

The Beginning...

One night Ellie was woken by a tapping at her window.

It was Robin the elf! "Would you like to go on an adventure?" he asked.

They flew above the rooftops. Soon they had arrived...

Contents

Jack Hassett (7) 72
Bethany Johnson (7) & Sophie 73

Our Lady Of Lourdes Catholic Primary School, Birkdale

Xander Wilson (7) 74
Iris Leonard (7) 76
Emma Oulton (7) 78
Guy Foster (7) 80
Lillia Dwan (7) 82
Harley Haywood (7) 84
Thomas Ralph (7) 86
Leon Kaye Carvalho (7) 87
Mia Bell (7) 88
Jasmine Wells 90
Poppy (7) 91
Payton Winning (7) 92
Milo Booth (6) 93
Robyn Bradley (7) 94
Jacob Givin (7) 95
Jessa Rose Shinto (7) 96
Emmy Duckworth (7) 97
Max Buttworth (7) 98
Kai Davidson (7) 99
Ave Maria 100
Emily Kate Hammond (7) 101
Jotham Oyedokun (7) 102
Sophie Monk (7) 103
Eva Serban (7) 104
Luke Latham (7) 105
Vincent Witter (7) 106
Reggie Hindle (6) 107

The Wickford CE School, Wickford

Hannah Natsai Jaratina (6) 108
Ralphie W (6) 109
Valerie Pinkovska (6) 110
Luca Jones (6) 111
Calla (6) 112
Prarthana Sreedevi (5) 113
Jude Vince (6) 114

Poppy Crittenden (6) 115
Sofia-Belle (6) 116
Kathleen Johnson (6) 117

Thorns Primary School, Quarry Bank

Forrest Harris (6) 118
Mason Jones (6) 120
Nevaeh Higginson (5) 121
Percy Jackson (6) 122
Bobby Simpson (6) 123
Ryan Sandland (6) 124
Willow Dunn (6) 125
Daisy Hadlington-Jones (6) 126
Georgia John (6) 127
Freya Hope (5) 128
Jorgie Cutler (6) 129
Daniel Berg (6) 130
Aurora Sangha (5) 131
Sofia Burgess (6) 132
Noah Prosser (6) 133

West Pelton Primary School, Stanley

Darcie-May Weldon (7) 134
Ben Robson (7) 136
Ellie Ramsey (6) 137
Aliya Docherty (6) 138
Ayla Tiffen (6) 139
Scarlett Pears (6) 140
Archie Brannen (5) 141
Shay Thomas (6) 142
Ruby Brown (6) 143
Terry Joe Oakes (6) 144
Joe Brown (6) 145
Joe Addison (5) 146

The Stories

Sehrish's Wonderland Adventure

Soon they arrived at Elf Wonderland. "Wow, look at this place," said Ellie.

"I know," said the elf.

"Wait, where's the king?" said Ellie.

"Oh I don't know where he is," replied the elf in horror.

They searched and searched and searched. "Oh no," said Ellie. "Where could he have gone?"

They walked to the bush and found the king hurt. "Are you okay, your majesty?" asked Ellie.

"Fine, I guess," replied the king.

After that they were walking back to the kingdom happily. "Yay, thank you," said the king.

"You're welcome."

They finally arrived at the kingdom and rejoiced. The girl then decided to live with them forever.

Sehrish Raza-Rizvi (7)

Granard Primary School, Putney

Royah's Pirate Adventure

Robin was taking Ellie to Pirate Island in a small wooden boat. Ellie took her favourite teddy with her on her adventure. Ellie was nervous but excited at the same time.

Robin showed Elie the treasure chest full of gold. She jumped on the trunk. "Arrr, I'm the richest girl in the world!" she said.

"You mean, we are the richest children in the world!" Robin interrupted.

Soon they saw a shadow in the distance. They looked closer and saw a fat, ugly pirate running towards them. He shouted, "Arrr, what are you doing on my island? Don't touch my golden box!"

The pirate took the chest and the children on the ship. "I will show you what pirates do with naughty children like you! Do you fancy walking the plank?" he asked.

"No, no! Help!" cried Robin and Ellie.

First Robin walked the plank and in the blink of an eye, he saw a dolphin. He whispered, "Help us please!"

Suddenly two dolphins came and rescued the kids. "Hooray!"

"That was a scary adventure!" said Ellie.

"I hope we don't see that ugly pirate again," said Robin.

The children went home. Do you think they might go on another adventure?

Royah Rian (7)
Granard Primary School, Putney

Radel's Space Adventure

Ellie and Robin, the aliens, were in space. They collected some stars along the way but they didn't spot the monster.

When they did, they were worried the monster would eat them.

Later the aliens could hear the monster's tummy rumbling. Then they got into their spaceship.

They flew down closer to the planet and couldn't believe it when they saw something. Can you guess what it was?

Of course, it was the monster! He stuck his tongue out, but the aliens drove their spaceship as fast as they could. The monster wasn't fast enough to catch them. They whizzed through space and after a while Ellie was home as they arrived. Ellie said goodbye to Robin and went to bed.

Radel Aliullov (6)

Granard Primary School, Putney

Matilda's Jungle Adventure

They arrived at a zoo and on the way in they swung on some vines that they spotted.
While they were swinging on the vines, they saw a witch that turned into a snake.
They both were so scared of the snake that Ellie and Robin ran away from the snake.
When Ellie and Robin thought they were safe, they spotted a lion. The lion asked if they would like a ride home and the children said, "Sure!"
They got off the lion's back and the children asked, "Where are you taking us?"
The lion said, "I'm taking you to Ellie's house!"
The lion took them to the vines and they swung home and when Ellie got back to her house she went back to sleep.

Matilda Bolt (7)
Granard Primary School, Putney

Elijah's Adventure Story

They found a tiny island, Ellie was amazed. She saw that everything was tiny.

She found a city and said to Robin, "Let's explore this city!"

Robin said, "Yes!"

They explored the city and Robin came across a large structure. Ellie asked, "What is this building?"

"It's Big Ben," said Robin.

Ellie found a village and she saw a funfair.

"Can we go on some rides?" asked Ellie.

They bought tokens and went on the slide.

Robin said, "We have to end this trip."

Robin made a portal and they went through it.

Elijah Warren (6)

Granard Primary School, Putney

Alana's Zoo Adventure

At the zoo, they saw an elephant who could talk. He said, "Just come in and I will take you on a ride?"
So they climbed aboard and the elephant took them to a bamboo forest. The elephant said, "You can get off now."
"Hey, what are you doing here? You are supposed to be living in China?"
Then they climbed back onto the elephant's back and they went to meet a monkey.
As soon as they met the monkey, he gave them a banana each and left.
Then they left the zoo and said goodbye to each other and hopped off the elephant's back.

Alana Warren (6)

Granard Primary School, Putney

Olaf's Magical Forest Adventure

In the middle of a city in a magical forest. Ellie had never seen such a colourful forest before.

In the forest they met friendly animals that led them to a mossy cave. They saw fog coming out of the cave.

The animals gave Ellie a stick. Ellie jumped in the hole and Robin watched from above. In front of Ellie there was a tree monster.

The tree monster threw acorns and sticks with swords, breaking Ellie's stick and Robin was stuck by the branches.

Ellie grabbed two stones from the floor and made a spark. They burned the monster and helped Ellie out.

Olaf Wolny (7)

Granard Primary School, Putney

Isabelle's Space Adventure

Soon they arrived in space.

When they finally arrived in space, they were looking at the sky and were having fun. Suddenly, there was an alien.

When Robin needed to do something, the alien took Ellie on his spaceship to explore space.

The alien and Ellie forgot about Robin.

"Where's Robin?" Ellie asked.

When they were searching for Robin, they found him on the moon.

"Robin," said Ellie. Suddenly there was a monster so they quickly went back to Earth. It was time to say goodbye to Ellie so she could sleep.

Isabelle Takyi (6)

Granard Primary School, Putney

Saad's Zoo Adventure

Robin the elf went to the zoo and they saw an elephant and they stared at it.

Then they rode the elephant. They enjoyed the ride very much. A small teddy bear was also riding on the elephant. There were also some plants.

Then Robin the elf went to a giant panda and the panda was holding a teddy and the teddy was hugging a girl.

Robin the elf went on a big elephant with his friend and explored the zoo.

Then his friends met a tall monkey who was holding a yellow banana.

In the end, Robin the elf waved goodbye.

Saad Rena (7)

Granard Primary School, Putney

Maissa's Magical Adventure

They flew so high and they flew to space. They saw a space unicorn who took them down to the sun.

On the sun, they saw a dragon and it breathed fire at them so they ran and ran and ran!

They met a little bear and he was so fast so they held his hands and zoomed off with him.

They jumped on the space unicorn and went to the moon. What will they see next?

They met a sneaky, old witch and they immediately ran off for no reason.

They snatched her broom and said goodbye to the unicorn. They then zoomed back home.

Maissa Berkemel (7)

Granard Primary School, Putney

Joaquim's Pirate Adventure

They arrived on a river and travelled on a small boat. The sun was shining. The water was calm.

Robin and Ellie discovered a grand treasure chest on a stranded island. It was astonishing.

Next they met a helpful pirate called Joe who opened the grand treasure chest. He also gave them a ride.

On the ride, Robin was about to fall off the plank and leave the boat.

They then started riding home on cyan dolphins.

Finally Robin and Ellie arrived home. Ellie was now ready for her comfy bed.

Joaquim Turkson (7)

Granard Primary School, Putney

Ernest's Zoo Adventure

The elf and Ellie flew to the zoo to look at the animals.

Ellie and the elf found an elephant and they got on his back.

After that, Ellie and the elf found a baby panda and Ellie and the panda hugged each other.

After that, Ellie and the elf got on the elephant to find more animals.

Then Ellie and the elf found a gorilla eating a banana.

Finally the elf and the elephant brought Ellie back home and said goodbye.

Ernest Starzyk (7)
Granard Primary School, Putney

Leo's Magical Adventure

Robin the elf introduced Ellie to his friend Uni the unicorn.

Suddenly they bumped into the aggressive dragon.

They were very scared and managed to get away from the dragon.

Ellie, Robin and Uni were finally enjoying their day after that crazy experience.

They came across a witch but she was a good witch...

The witch borrowed her broomstick so Robin and Ellie could get home.

Leo Westwood (7)

Granard Primary School, Putney

Michael's Magical Adventure

When they got there they swung high and far until they met a... snake!

The snake wanted to eat them. "Argh!"

"Run away!"

They ran and ran until they lost the snake.

"Phew, we almost got caught!"

Soon they met a lion, it was a kind lion.

"I will take you home," said the lion.

They swung on vines and went home.

Michael Moss (6)

Granard Primary School, Putney

Olivia's Magical Adventure

The boy and the girl got on a unicorn and flew off.

They got off the unicorn and saw a dragon in front of them and they ran off.

A teddy bear ran off with the boy and the girl.

The girl picked up the bear and got on with the bear and the boy.

They got off and a cheeky elf came and took them but they got out.

They found a broom and rode home.

Olivia Baden (7)

Granard Primary School, Putney

Chloe's Zoo Adventure

They flew to the zoo.

They met an elephant and hopped on the elephant.

The elephant took them to a panda and they hugged the panda.

They hopped back on the elephant and he took them to the monkeys.

One monkey was very cheeky and ate lots of bananas.

The elephant took them both home and Ellie went to bed.

Chloe Sullivan (6)

Granard Primary School, Putney

Kaley-Flora's First Story

Once upon a time, there was a girl and a boy and they were sailing in a dusty brown boat. Then they saw a pretty island so they went off.

Suddenly, they saw a pirate and the girl and boy said, "Who are you?"

The pirate said, "I am a nice kind pirate."

The girl said, "We are looking for the treasure."

The pirate said, "I am looking for the treasure too."

They went to find the sparkly, shiny treasure, but there was a deep, scary cave! The girl said, "Why is there a cave on the island?"

Then they saw the treasure and they couldn't believe their eyes. They saw a monster and he grabbed the children and the pirate fought the huge scary monster, the pirate kicked him in the eye and he died. The girl and the boy were happy, but it was late and they had to go home.

The pirate said goodbye to the girl and the boy and they went back to the brown, dusty boat and they finally arrived home. They lived happily ever after.

Kaley-Flora Escobar Nogueira (6)

Harris Primary Free School Peckham, Peckham

Alaia's First Story

Once upon a time, there was a little girl called Goldilocks. Her mum didn't want her to go to the forest, it was so scary, but she went to the scary forest. Then she saw a big bad wolf, he asked, "Where are you going, young lady?" She said to her grandmother's so the wolf ran to her grandmother's. The wolf gobbled the grandmother up and the wolf acted like the grandmother and when Goldilocks came in she didn't notice. The wolf's belly started to hurt so he took the grandmother out of his belly, then the grandmother hugged Goldilocks. The grandmother knocked the wolf out and Goldilocks was so happy. Then Goldilocks' mum came, she was so sad she had gone in the scary forest. Her mum had found her and said, "I will never let you go in the forest again!" They lived happily ever after.

Alaia Gore (7)

Harris Primary Free School Peckham, Peckham

Zara's First Story

One day, Bell went with her brother, they were both magnificent fairies and they flew across the rooftops and landed at a legendary golden castle.

A kind, smart wizard helped them make a potion to make a pet rabbit, but the wizard's brother was an evil and smart wizard. He threw the rabbit out of the window but the rabbit didn't die. The bad wizard realised what he had done and rushed down the stairs and picked up the cute little rabbit.

They all walked home, Bell and her brother went one way and the wizards went another. They took each other's numbers and called each other all the time. They lived happily ever after.

Zara Ikere (6)

Harris Primary Free School Peckham, Peckham

Maria's First Story

They landed on some grass and saw golden pretty flowers and a bus that went past big mountains. There was a kind polar bear and they wanted to be friends.

Then they went to find a caterpillar but he was stuck in a huge cage. They helped him and he got out. They found a beautiful fox and she was sleeping on the mountain. They found a worm and he was stuck, so they helped him get out and pop! He went with them.

They took all the animals home and lived happily ever after.

Maria Ihtesham (7)

Harris Primary Free School Peckham, Peckham

Sebastian's Pirate Adventure

Luckily, they arrived in the middle of the ocean. They found some treasure in a golden treasure chest. A pirate came, oh no! The pirate made them walk the plank. Some dolphins rescued them. Then they lived happily ever after.

Sebastian Sarmiento

Harris Primary Free School Peckham, Peckham

Erik's Pirate Adventure

The children were on a boat. They found a beautiful treasure chest. A pirate ship appeared - oh no! The pirates made them walk the plank. Then some dolphins rescued them. They lived happily eve after.

Erik Raizuehtu (7)

Harris Primary Free School Peckham, Peckham

Matthew's Adventure

As they were flying over the houses, Ellie saw the world change. It changed into a jungle and a lion spotted them.

They soared over the jungle and when they landed the lion told the other lions that intruders had come. When Ellie and Robin didn't know.

When the lions came back they realised that they had to run very far. When the lions saw Ellie and Robin in sight they ran faster. Then Ellie saw the lions and shouted, "The lions are chasing us!" to the magical elf. Just then the lions were really close to them. Robin used his magic to make a tree fall down and the lions stopped running to get to Ellie and Robin.

Then Ellie felt herself flying again. Then Ellie saw the world change again as they were flying over and Ellie was back home.

Matthew Leonard (7)

High Wycombe CE Combined School, High Wycombe

Mofiyinfoluwa's Adventure

...at a deep dark forest. Once Ellie and Robin got back on the ground, Ellie told Robin to look at her side and once Robin saw it Robin was shocked in amazement. Robin couldn't believe his eyes. He saw the most beautiful and rarest thing in the world, it was a four-leaf clover.

Soon they reached the most beautiful garden full of four-leaf clovers but they all started to become weeds. Robin and Ellie were shocked at what they just saw.

Robin forgot to tell Ellie something, he forgot to tell her about fairies. Robin remembered telling Ellie that fairies were going to introduce them to the land of flowers. Robin told her and Ellie was excited but she had no clue what to do when she saw one. She was nervous that the fairies wouldn't like her. Robin said not to worry about a thing.

Ellie took a deep breath in and out three times. Robin was very sure that it was going to be fine but he didn't think that the evil fairy Jack Hot was going to come out from the evil portal. Jack Hot was very lazy, jealous and angry. Things weren't going according to plan.

Robin made a loud whistle and suddenly there came the thinnest broom Ellie had ever seen. Robin explained that he knew what Jack Hot was looking for. "What is he looking for?" asked Ellie.

Robin replied, "He is looking for a golden ball which grants any wish you want."

Ellie replied, "Really?"

"We're off to find it!"

They found it in the middle of the forest behind some bushes. Ellie was feeling a bit sleepy so in a wink of an eye she was sleeping in her bed.

Mofiyinfoluwa Olorode (7)

High Wycombe CE Combined School, High Wycombe

Claudia's Adventure

Ellie opened her eyes and saw the most mesmerising thing! In front of her were hundreds of pixies. It was Pixie Land!

Robin cried, "Where's my wand?" and Ellie turned to see a figure running away. "I recognise that moustache," panicked Robin, "that's Michael the Malicious!" They tried to run after him, but were too tired.

Robin and Ellie staggered through the door of the nearest wand shop and shouted for the shopkeeper. Robin panted, "I need a wand!" and Ellie explained what had happened.

"Right-oh!" said the shopkeeper. "I'm sure I have one." And he was soon back with a shiny wand.

Ellie grabbed it and ran outside. Closing one eye, Ellie focused on the figure of Michael the Malicious in the distance. She gracefully swirled the wand, and sang, "Hibady, hilaby, hidaby doo, I'm sending an iceberg just to freeze you!"

To her amazement, out of the tip of the wand appeared a silvery arrow which shot towards Michael. It touched his arm and he froze, just like an iceberg!

Ellie and Robin danced a happy dance and then took Michael to the police. After all that, there was only one thing left to do - party! They danced, sang and ate pixie cakes.

Ellie fell asleep in a cosy armchair while the music swirled around her, getting fainter and fainter... and fainter.

She woke up in her own bed and thought she'd been dreaming, but then she looked under her pillow and saw a tiny pixie armchair. It wasn't a dream after all!

Claudia Mason (7)

High Wycombe CE Combined School, High Wycombe

Annabel's Magical Story

...at Pixie Land! They saw a magical unicorn called Izzy. She had a blue mane with beautiful deep purple skin. Ellie was feeling enchanted when riding on the magical unicorn.

Suddenly, Boris appeared! Boris was a big, flamey dragon who scared Ellie's teddy bear called Bob. Ellie felt terrified too. Robin was mad at the dragon for scaring his friends. Robin and Ellie knew that they could outrun the dragon because he was very lazy and never practised his running skills. So they ran for their lives!

They ran so fast that they caught up with Izzy Moonbow, their very best unicorn friend. Even though they were with Izzy they still felt terrified of big bad Boris.

Izzy took them to Lollipop Land where they found Glinda the witch. They started off being scared of Glinda but found out that she was a good witch who gave them her wooden broomstick.

Robin, Ellie and Bob used the wooden broomstick to climb on and get out of Pixie Land. They flew home where they were safe and sound. Ellie climbed back in bed and said goodnight to Robin.

Annabel Connelly (7)

High Wycombe CE Combined School, High Wycombe

Khalia's Magical Adventure

They flew above the rooftops with the help of a magical flying unicorn.

Ellie and Robin came across the fire-breathing dragon from the Sleeping Beauty story. They tried to speak to the dragon thinking maybe they could be his friend because he seemed to be so lonely. But he didn't want to be friends so he decided to blow a massive fireball right at them. "Run!" Luckily, Rainbow Sparkly came to the rescue and away they flew as fast as they could from the scary dragon.

Robin and Ellie then came across a witch standing outside a house made of colourful, fizzy and mouth-popping candy. This witch wasn't the mean horrible witch from the Hansel and Gretel story, this witch was nice. She showed them how to make their own sweets.

Once they finished this wonderful adventure it was time for Ellie to go home back to bed.

"Goodbye Robin," said Ellie. "I can't wait to tell Mummy, Daddy and my sister about our adventure."
"Until next time," said Robin.

Khalia Lexa Blackwood (6)
High Wycombe CE Combined School, High Wycombe

Anna's Adventure

It had been a long journey. It was like a conga in the sky because Robin was flying and holding onto Ellie and Ellie was holding onto Buffy her dog.

To Ellie it seemed that the journey was five hours but soon they landed in a gingerbread land. Everything was made out of gingerbread! It smelt of sweets and freshly baked cookies.

Everything was edible! They all grabbed a piece of gingerbread and gobbled it up. They all started looking for more food. It was very peaceful, no noise and no trouble until they saw a gigantic house. In the house they saw an old lady that said to them, "Come in, come in, I won't hurt you!" But it was a trick! The old lady was a witch and she locked Robin in a cage. Buffy and Ellie tried to get Robin out but it would not work.

Finally Ellie kicked the witch out and took the keys from her. She unlocked the door and Robin was free once more! They flew back to Ellie's room and the witch was never seen again.

Anna Horne (7)

High Wycombe CE Combined School, High Wycombe

Sofia's Magical Adventure

In the New Forest Ellie, Robin and Little Ted found a unicorn in the woods and asked if they could have a ride. The unicorn said, "Yes," so they rode to a magical place called Imaginary Land.

When they got there they saw a scaly, scary, fiery dragon! They were terrified! It was the biggest dragon they'd ever seen. "Quick, let's use our special whistle to call for help." They started to run as fast as they could. Little Ted could feel the dragon's hot flamey breath. Would they make it in time?

Luckily, their unicorn friend heard their whistle and came to the rescue. They flew high over the clouds and saw a beautiful and bright rainbow in the sky. When they looked down they saw a very big house with tasty, colourful sweets in the front garden. A kind and friendly witch came out and gave them a broomstick to fly on.

Once home, Ellie jumped into bed and quickly drifted off to sleep, dreaming about her magical adventure.

Sofia Justice (7)

High Wycombe CE Combined School, High Wycombe

Isabella's Magical Story

They came to a lovely island! The place was full of big green trees. There was also a path that led to a dark gloomy cave. They went in... closer and closer until they saw a bit of fire. Then the beast was revealed, it was a green old dragon... oh no!

They ran away fast. When the children got out they looked behind them. He was still there. They ran into the big thick bushes. Then they saw something come closer. The animal was revealed and it was a golden-horned unicorn. *Clip-clop, clip-clop.* The children jumped up onto the unicorn's back, but the children saw something...

The unicorn ran away. It was a witch, a green witch! Robin distracted the witch whilst Ellie got the broomstick.

They flew over the horrible witch then over the thick bush where the unicorn was, over the dragon cave, then they saw home.

When they got there Ellie went through the window and they lived happily ever after.

Isabella Ross (6)
High Wycombe CE Combined School, High Wycombe

Ezra's Pirate Adventure

They flew to the dock and found a little wooden boat. Ellie jumped into it and Robin rowed. Teddy was confused so Ellie cuddled him tight.

Finally they made it to an island. They found a chest full of gold and silver. Teddy put on a small crown and danced around and pretended he was a king.

Robin spotted a pirate ship! The pirate ship came to shore. "Arrr!" said Pirate Pete and tied up Ellie and Robin. Teddy clung to Robin's leg like a sloth.

Pirate Pete took them to his ship and made them walk the plank. He thought they were going to steal his treasure! But Robin spotted a dolphin and called in a secret language.

The dolphin called his friend and rescued Robin, Ellie and Teddy. They happily swam to shore.

In the middle of the night, they walked quietly along a path to Ellie's house. They talked all about their amazing adventure.

Ezra Stocks (7)

High Wycombe CE Combined School, High Wycombe

Mele's Adventure

They landed in an enchanted forest where they heard birds chirping and saw fairies flying above their heads.

As they started exploring they found a phoenix sitting in a tree eating magical cookies with fairy dust on them.

Ellie was too busy looking around that she accidentally lost Robin! She was so scared. "Oh no, I don't know what to do!" cried Ellie. When she finally thought of an idea, she kept on saying to herself, "If I were Robin, where would I go?" And using that strategy she found Robin!

She was so happy when she found him and after she told him all about how she found Robin, they continued on their journey.

Even crazier stuff was in the forest. A mermaid on the floor flopping about. They helped her get back in the water and kept on exploring.

Mele Rushton (7)

High Wycombe CE Combined School, High Wycombe

Taylon's Pirate Adventure

Ellie and Robin found a boat and sailed across the sea to an island to find treasure. They found an island and they dug some holes and discovered a treasure chest. It was locked and they found a key to open it up.

A pirate came out of nowhere and opened it up together. There were coins, necklaces and diamonds and the pirate raised his sword up and said, "It's my treasure, now you are coming to my ship. Walk the plank both of you before I slice you both up!" They listened to the pirate and dolphins came to the rescue. The dolphins took Ellie and Robin to land.

Ellie and Robin walked all the way from the island to their house and had some food and went to bed and they lived happily ever after.

Taylon Woods-Cardoso (7)

High Wycombe CE Combined School, High Wycombe

Tiago's Pirate Adventure

They stopped on the shore. They climbed up a coconut tree and found an X marking the spot. They dug with their hands and hit a treasure chest.

Then Robin the elf saw a moving monkey toy. Ellie was standing on the chest holding a crown and waving.

The pirate said, "Oi you stop stealing my treasure or else I will make you walk the plank."

"I'm not scared of you."

"Fine, you didn't listen to me, now you have to walk the plank. Bye, Robin the elf and you little girl."

"I don't want to."

A dolphin saved them. They were happy and excited because they survived and were having fun riding the dolphin.

They lived happily ever after.

Tiago Woods-Cardoso (7)

High Wycombe CE Combined School, High Wycombe

Bella's Magical Adventure

Soon they arrived in an enchanted forest. They stepped off the magical unicorn onto the soft green grass.

Suddenly, out of nowhere, a huge fire-breathing dragon roared in their faces very loudly. They were horrified.

Robin, Ellie and her teddy ran as fast as they could away from the scary fire-breathing dragon!

Robin whistled for the unicorn to come so they could go faster than the evil dragon.

The unicorn took them to Lolly Land where they met a tricky old witch. They quickly ran into her lollipop house and they took the witch's broomstick.

They quickly ran out the witch's door and hopped on the broomstick ready to go home and they lived happily ever after.

Bella Stott (7)

High Wycombe CE Combined School, High Wycombe

Phoebe's Magical Adventure

Ellie and Robin flew on a bright pink and white unicorn which had a sparkly horn. They softly landed on the ground. Suddenly there were big loud thumps. They turned around and it was a giant dragon! A big and scary dragon with a fierce look on its face. Ellie and Robin turned quickly and ran as fast as they could.

They ran back to the unicorn and Ellie picked her teddy bear up and they jumped on. The unicorn took off high up into the sky.

They saw a candy kingdom and landed with hardly a bump. Then they heard a voice, it was a wicked witch...

The witch turned round and Robin spotted a broomstick. Then Ellie said, "How about we use it to fly home?"

Phoebe Clark (7)

High Wycombe CE Combined School, High Wycombe

Jonah's Pirate Story

They went on an old rickety wooden boat to an island. Robin rowed and rowed until they were at the island.

"Treasure!" yelled the teddy bear and grabbed a crown. "I am King Bob!"

"Uh oh," shouted Robin. "Pirates!"

Captain Golden Hook saw the glimmering treasure. "I'll be having that!" he said furiously.

He snatched the treasure and made Robin, Ellie and King Bob walk the plank. They tiptoed on the plank and fell off and nearly touched the water. Suddenly dolphins rescued them.

They quickly swam back to land, saw their house and walked to it.

Jonah Wells (6)

High Wycombe CE Combined School, High Wycombe

Alexander's Jungle Adventure

Soon they arrived at the jungle. "It is so cool!" Ellie said.

Ellie and Teddy swung on vines so fast that they were feeling dizzy.

Suddenly a fierce python appeared by them. It was so long that it was longer than the vines! The python was immediately going to eat Robin and Ellie. They ran as fast as they could.

Soon they came across a friendly lion. The two children kindly asked if it could take them home. The lion did what they asked. They zoomed across the jungle.

Unfortunately they had to go home so they swung on vines out of the jungle and flew back home.

Alexander Veverka (7)

High Wycombe CE Combined School, High Wycombe

Zachary's Adventure

They arrived at a mysterious island where they needed to find a specific, rare football. The island was vast and lonely because there were no people. They searched high and low even through the tree branches and then... they finally found it!
But the location was wedged in a mountain. So they had to bang it open. Luckily they found two hammers just lying around. They made a hole big enough to fit through and they got hold of it...
As soon as they got out they saw people running towards them. But they were safe because Robin flew them to safety.

Zachary Phillip (7)

High Wycombe CE Combined School, High Wycombe

Andrey's Jungle Story

When they arrived, Robin the elf said, "Would you like to swing on some vines?" Ellie replied, "Yes!"

When they were finished a snake came. Ellie was scared but knew what to do - run! He chased them. They were running so fast that Ellie forgot about the snake.

They stopped and saw a big fierce lion. The lion said, "Jump on my back and I will take you home." The lion was running so fast because he wanted to get to the window. When they arrived at Ellie's home she crept through the window. She thought it was a dream!

Andrey Ivanov (7)

High Wycombe CE Combined School, High Wycombe

Thea's Adventure

Ellie asked Robin, "Where are we?"
Robin said, "We are in Egypt." Down below them were pyramids.
Ellie and Robin saw a gemstone. Then they saw a wall. They put the gemstone in the wall. The wall lifted up. Ellie and Robin walked in the secret cave. Uh oh, there was a mummy!
The mummy chased them. They felt very scared. "What are we going to do?"
As Ellie and Robin ran they pulled the gemstone out. As the mummy ran after them the wall crashed on the mummy. They were safe.

Thea Jonsmyth-Clarke (6)
High Wycombe CE Combined School, High Wycombe

Ellis's Adventure

...in the hottest place on Earth! The Sahara Desert. When they arrived they looked for food.

A few minutes later they found a hundred kangaroos. They thought they were lost. Ellie ran over to the kangaroos and then asked them if they were okay. They shook their heads.

Ellie made a plan and asked Robin to help the kangaroos fly home.

They formed a line then Robin waved his hand then they all flew to Australia.

Then they said bye to each other and Robin and Ellie went home themselves.

Ellis Thomas (6)

High Wycombe CE Combined School, High Wycombe

Kristen's Magical Story

Ellie and Robin the elf were in an enchanted forest that could grant wishes. Ellie made a wish but... it made a dragon!

"Argh!" Ellie and Robin had to run away.

Then they ran away to the secret destination. They went back to their magical unicorn in the enchanted woods. Ellie and Robin went to a mysterious witch that sold poisonous candy to their teddy bear. But he was fine afterwards.

Then Ellie and Robin got to Ellie's house and said goodbye.

Kristen Mendoza (7)

High Wycombe CE Combined School, High Wycombe

Zain's Jungle Adventure

Ellie and Robin were swinging on the ropes with a teddy bear.

They were looking at the snake and they were scared and frightened. Ellie and Robin ran because the snake was scary.

The tiger was feeling happy and Ellie and Robin were thinking.

They were running and happy. They were swinging on ropes and went home.

Zain Farooq (6)

High Wycombe CE Combined School, High Wycombe

Micah's Pirate Adventure

Robin the elf and Ellie went on an adventure to the sea.

Soon they got to Bimbre Island and found treasure!

Suddenly Mr Grumpy the pirate stole the treasure. Then Mr Grumpy the pirate made them walk the plank.

Suddenly when they dropped, two dolphins dived to save them.

Finally they arrived at home.

Micah James (7)

High Wycombe CE Combined School, High Wycombe

Abdul's Pirate Adventure

They sailed to an island.

When they arrived at the island they found a chest and they saw a pirate ship.

The pirate came to the island and took them to the ship. The pirate told them to walk the plank, but they landed on a dolphin.

Then they went home.

Abdul Sohail (6)

High Wycombe CE Combined School, High Wycombe

Julian's Jungle Adventure

Ellie and Robin went in the jungle but... snake! But it was kind. They asked it where they were.

Then the snake tried to eat them but they ran away.

Then they met a lion called Snap. He helped them. They rode Snap then...

Next Ellie quickly went home.

Julian Stawicki (7)

High Wycombe CE Combined School, High Wycombe

Alex's Jungle Story

They were hanging on the vine. They saw a snake. They were scared.
They ran because they were scared.
The tiger was kind with the kids. The tiger took the kids on its back. They went home.

Alex Constantin (7)

High Wycombe CE Combined School, High Wycombe

Barley's Adventure

...in a magical, wonderful, amazing place. They saw flowers everywhere. They were so amazed. It looked like a colourful rainbow.

"We love it! But what shall we do?"

Next, they saw a parade with balloons. It was a wonderful and colourful parade. There were lovely drinks, gorgeous cookies and cakes.

The next day... "Ellie! Ellie!"

"Yes, Robin?"

"I've got a new job!"

"What is it?"

"It, it, it, it's working at the doughnut place!"

"Let's go then!"

They were at the doughnut place. An alarm came on. She didn't know why, so she just carried on doing her work. It was the fire alarm!

Suddenly, there were loads of robbers. She was put in a sack in a *snap!* She was screaming, "Argh! Help me, please!"

Robin heard her and ran to help. He ran and got her. "Well, that's a relief."
"Ellie, do you have something to say?"
"Thank you."

Barley Blackwell (7)
Ospringe CE Primary School, Ospringe

Bethany's Jungle Adventure

In a magical, rainy, green rainforest, Ellie and Robin were wondering how they would be able to get home. Then they met a girl who had a panda. Her name was Lola. After Robin had met Lola, he said, "Do you know the way home?" Suddenly, Lola turned into a snake. "Oh, Ellie! D-d-d-do you think we said the wrong thing?" Next, Lola started to chase them.

"I think we said a word that turns her into a snake. I think the word was 'way'. That word turned her into a green, slimy, gooey snake."

Lola led them to a lion. They thought they could ride it to get back home. They checked that it was a friendly lion and it was, so they decided to tell it the way home. When they were on their way home, they realised that Lola was still chasing them. They hid in a bush so Lola couldn't find them.

When Lola had left, they jumped off the lion and said, "Thank you." Then they swung on the vines all the way home.

Bethany Holbrook (7)

Ospringe CE Primary School, Ospringe

Connor's Adventure

There was a boy called Jack. He was a very cheeky boy. His mum and dad were concerned. They didn't know where he was. He kept walking until he came to the Eiffel Tower. Jack was shocked. He went much closer. He thought it was intense. *What am I looking at?* he said to himself. A mansion! There were so many things, including a swimming pool. It was intense. He was gasping. *How did I come across this?* He was rich! It was a great home. He went back outside the house and he was a bit scared when he heard footsteps in the forest. There was a yucky swamp. *How did I come across this? Why is there a police station here now? How amazing!*

Connor Reeves (7)

Ospringe CE Primary School, Ospringe

Lily-Marie's Magical Adventure

...in a magical land.

They met a shiny, beautiful, magical unicorn and she lived in the rainbow rainforest.

Next, they found a dragon and then the dragon breathed fire and the unicorn disappeared.

Next, they ran because the dragon breathed big flames. So they ran away to find the unicorn. Then they found the unicorn and they celebrated for half an hour.

Next, they found a cottage made out of candy and it had a warning on it. It said: 'Do not eat this house, a witch lives inside'.

Lastly, they went home. They used the witch's broom to fly home.

Lily-Marie Higgs (7)

Ospringe CE Primary School, Ospringe

Harry's Adventure

...in a wonderful, amazing land.

Ellie wanted to explore the wonderful land. She saw a magical unicorn that had magnificent wings.

Next, she got on the magical unicorn and flew away. They went to another island that was creepy and dark. They explored the dark and creepy place and they saw skeletons everywhere.

Then they saw a big, dark shadow. Then they saw a big, black dragon. They tried to run away but they got caught. Suddenly, a baby bear fought the big, black dragon.

Next, the baby bear defeated the dragon. Finally, the bear, Ellie and Robin had done it.

Harry Harris (7)

Ospringe CE Primary School, Ospringe

Reggie's Adventure

Once upon a time, there was a square guy named Blocky and he lived in Cartoon World. No one knew what he looked like, but now you know!

Blocky told his mum to use the Teleport 6000 to teleport him to the jungle! She said, "Okay, you can go."

When he got to the jungle, he met SpongeBob!

He said, "Hi!"

And Blocky said, "Hi!" back.

But SpongeBob was evil! Before SpongeBob could beat him, a glitch happened. *Glitch warning!* Blocky won and SpongeBob lost. It was the end of SpongeBob.

Reggie Hampton (7)
Ospringe CE Primary School, Ospringe

Toby's Jungle Adventure

...in the jungle!

Ellie found a baby bear. The baby bear ran away. They swung onwards. They landed by a snake.

"Why are you here?" asked the snake.

"Um... um... um!" said Ellie.

"Let's leave!" said Robin.

They saw another snake. They had to run. They escaped. Suddenly, a lion pounced out of a bush. They screamed, but the lion was friendly.

They played and played until it was night. They swung back home. Ellie had a good night's sleep.

Toby Cassell (7)

Ospringe CE Primary School, Ospringe

Mia's Zoo Adventure

...at the zoo.

Ellie and Robin arrived at the zoo. They were so excited. The first thing they saw was an elephant. They rode on the elephant, who was very happy.

After, they saw a panda and they hugged the panda. Then she rode the elephant again with her teddy and Robin. Then they met a monkey. He shared his banana with them.

After a long night at the zoo, Robin took Ellie home.

Mia Wallace (6)

Ospringe CE Primary School, Ospringe

Isla's Jungle Adventure

Once upon a time, Ellie and Robin went to the jungle. They swung on the branches. While they were walking through the jungle, they saw a snake. It was scary. They were scared, so they ran as fast as they could. While they were in the jungle, they saw a tiger. The tiger jumped out of the bushes and they nearly got eaten by the tiger. They swung out of the jungle.

Isla Harris (7)

Ospringe CE Primary School, Ospringe

Sophie's Magical Adventure

Once upon a time, Ellie and Robin went to the forest. Then they saw a unicorn and they rode the unicorn. Then a dragon appeared and it was angry. They were scared.

Then the dragon breathed fire and they got even more scared. Suddenly, the unicorn saved them!

Then the witch said, "You can use my broomstick."

Then they used it and they went home.

Sophie Jayes (7)
Ospringe CE Primary School, Ospringe

Jack's Adventure

Tie was hanging out of his window when a man popped out from nowhere. Tie was so confused. The man said, "Come here!"
Tie was eating a bagel on the Eiffel Tower! Tie was singing and then the crowd shouted, "Boo!" He left and cried.
Tie carried on crying and then it started raining. Tie signed up for an FBI job. He was happy there.

Jack Hassett (7)
Ospringe CE Primary School, Ospringe

Our Adventure

Once upon a time, there was a boy and a girl. They were playing outside on the slide. They went to school and there was a bully. The bully cut the girl's hair. She and her brother ran home as fast as they could. They told their parents and went to bed.

Bethany Johnson (7) & Sophie

Ospringe CE Primary School, Ospringe

Xander's Adventure

...in the jungle.

Robin told Ellie that the secret tomb was nearby. They ventured through the jungle until they came across some rubble from a broken-down temple. Ellie looked around and spotted some cheeky monkeys looking for a snack. The monkeys saw some bananas in Ellie's backpack and when Robin and Ellie sat down for a rest, they zipped in and stole the backpack.

As the monkeys darted off, Robin and Ellie gave chase shouting, "Hey, that's my backpack!"

As they caught up with them, they stumbled through some vines and tumbled down into the tomb.

"The secret tomb!" gasped Robin.

Ellie replied, "We actually found it, thanks to those cheeky monkeys!"

On the wall was a series of puzzles they had to solve to get past all the traps. Robin and Ellie worked as a team and in no time, they were at the end of the tomb where a bright green emerald lay waiting for them.
Ellie said, "I think it's time I went home."
Ellie thanked Robin for the adventure and said, "Till next time, Robin..."

Xander Wilson (7)
Our Lady Of Lourdes Catholic Primary School, Birkdale

Iris' Adventure

...on their neighbour's roof.

A minute later, Ellie thought she should get some instruments. So she got a flute, a guitar and a violin, and then they skipped their way to the park.

As they dragged themselves through the park's entrance, they saw dazzling daisies, green grass and flowing flowers. They walked to the play area and found a rusty rocket. They started feeling a weird feeling.

"Robin, do you feel that too?"

They thought they were growing.

Soon, the floor dropped and they landed on the moon.

"Uh-oh!" said Robin.

They were tiptoeing by babies hiding in holes and walking past aliens. Soon, they saw a group of horse-frogs and a purple one screamed, "Intruders!"

"Uh- Ellie, we've got a problem," said Robin. There was fighting and punching and kicking! But finally, they won the war! Soon, they all agreed, "You have to serve us." The aliens took a UFO and got to their home first. But instead of making food, they burnt it down - Every. Last. Bit.

Iris Leonard (7)

Our Lady Of Lourdes Catholic Primary School, Birkdale

Emma's Adventure

...at a magical forest.

Ellie looked up and saw the tall, leafy, green, sparkly trees. Ellie was amazed and knew this was a special place. Robin asked Ellie to look for a missing unicorn. This unicorn was rare because it could teleport to different planets.

Robin whispered, "I think the goblins have got the unicorn."

Ellie and Robin set off to search for the unicorn. Ellie started to feel worried because she didn't know if the goblins were nasty. Robin held Ellie's hand.

Ellie and Robin found the goblins' cave. They could see the unicorn's light shining. Robin exclaimed, "I will distract the goblins while you unchain the unicorn!"

Ellie went into the cave. She waited for Robin to distract the goblin and ran over to the unicorn and quickly pulled the magnets and they ran away.

Robin ran over to Ellie and the unicorn. They were feeling happy but also worried because the goblins might get them. The unicorn used her teleportation powers and took Ellie home.

Emma Oulton (7)

Our Lady Of Lourdes Catholic Primary School, Birkdale

Guy's Space Adventure

...in space.

Ellie and Robin left Earth. They headed towards the stars. Earth looked so small in the distance. Ellie felt happy, joyful, trusted and relaxed with her elf friend.

They arrived on the moon and reached for the stars. Their feet felt cold on the icy moon. An alien was spying on them in the distance. He was controlling the spaceship. A yellow light shone down for Ellie and her teddy to join the alien for the ride of their life.

The alien told Ellie all about the stars.

"Go on... wish on a star!" squealed the alien.

"Wow, I never knew you could do that," whispered Ellie.

Now, with shocked faces, there was a giant alien with three eyes trying to take over the spaceship with a pink, slobbery tongue licking. They made their escape.

Now, the moon was back in the distance. Ellie's wish had come true! The spaceship got her and her teddy home safely to her mum and dad. Ellie and her new friends waved goodbye to each other.

Guy Foster (7)
Our Lady Of Lourdes Catholic Primary School, Birkdale

Lillia's Magical Adventure

...in a mysterious land.

A few seconds later, a colourful unicorn appeared beside them. They clambered on her back and they all disappeared.

In a flash of light, there was a fierce fire-breathing dragon. Ellie and Robin were terrified. The scary dragon came closer and closer to them.

Quickly, Ellie and Robin raced away with the mean dragon chasing them. They ran through a field of ice. The dragon slipped and the children got away.

From nowhere, the unicorn appeared again. The unicorn took them to a land of candy. There was a chocolate floor, marshmallow clouds and lollipop flowers.

As Ellie picked up a lollipop flower, a witch popped out. She was a nice witch.

"Are you lost?" asked the witch.

"Yes," said Ellie.

They told her everything.

The witch let them use her broomstick. They were really happy to be going home but there was one problem: How would they give back the broomstick...?

Lillia Dwan (7)

Our Lady Of Lourdes Catholic Primary School, Birkdale

Harley's Space Adventure

...in space. Ellie and Robin went to an adventure land where people got to fly and have peace with people.

"Robin? What is this place?" said Ellie.

When they got there, they looked at the shooting stars. While they were looking at the stars, an alien was spying on them. The alien took Ellie and Robin to her spaceship. The alien asked to be friends with them and Ellie's teddy.

Then the alien showed Ellie around the amazing world.

"Wow! This is awesome," Ellie said.

After they took a monster into the spaceship and the alien kept the monster as a pet.

Then the adventure was over. They talked for a little bit. Then she said goodbye.

The alien said, "Let's go out again sometime soon."
"Okay," Ellie said.

Harley Haywood (7)

Our Lady Of Lourdes Catholic Primary School, Birkdale

Thomas' Zoo Adventure

...at the zoo where animals roamed freely. There were mysterious animals from all over the world.

Mr Elephant kindly offered them a ride on his back. "Where would you like to go?" he asked.

"To the pandas, please," replied Ellie.

They were surprised to find a baby panda with its mummy. Ellie had a cuddle with the panda while Robin held the baby.

They climbed back onto Mr Elephant's back, ready to find another animal. Mr Elephant carried Ellie's teddy bear called Olive in his trunk.

They arrived where the chimpanzee lived. They enjoyed a yummy banana together.

"It's time to go home," said Robin.

Mr Elephant gave Ellie a lift home.

"Thank you for our adventure, Robin," said Ellie, waving goodbye.

Thomas Ralph (7)

Our Lady Of Lourdes Catholic Primary School, Birkdale

Leon's Adventure

...at a graveyard.

They flew over the graves and Jesus' cross. They landed and prayed in front of it.

Then they went to Tesco but it was still being built and the name was spelt like Tessxo.

They flew to Ellie's house and then Robin the elf flew back to his home.

The next day, Ellie went to Robin the elf's house but he was ill, so she played on her own. None of her games were fun now, not even her favourite game was enough without Robin the elf.

Two days later, Robin the elf was better and Ellie was happy again. They played football for most of the day and had an amazing adventure.

Leon Kaye Carvalho (7)

Our Lady Of Lourdes Catholic Primary School, Birkdale

Mia's Zoo Adventure

...at the zoo.

They arrived at the zoo. They saw many wonderful animals, such as enormous elephants, gigantic giraffes and a magic monkey.

The enormous elephant waited for Ellie and Robin to get on top. They got on the elephant and a baby panda came along for the ride.

The baby panda led the way to his family. They stayed there for an hour and left. He led the way again. This time, he led the way to a chimpanzee. On the way, they went past lots of curious animals.

They finally arrived and Robin ate a banana while the baby panda swung on a vine. Suddenly, Robin had to go home.

They calmly walked and settled on the elephant. They said goodbye and set off on their way home. They looked at the moon and said, "We'll have another trip soon."

Mia Bell (7)

Our Lady Of Lourdes Catholic Primary School, Birkdale

Jasmine's Magical Adventure

One night, Ellie went to sleep. But while she was asleep, she heard a knock at her window. It was Robin the elf. Robin told Ellie to come and see a unicorn.

When they got off the unicorn, they started walking and on the way, they saw a dragon. It was walking closer to them. Suddenly, they were running away from the dragon. Later, they found the cute unicorn. They all got on the unicorn. When they got off the unicorn, they saw a witch. The witch gave them a broom and ran away. They were scared but laughed at her.

Then they all got on the broom and went home. They lived happily ever after.

Jasmine Wells

Our Lady Of Lourdes Catholic Primary School, Birkdale

Poppy's Adventure

Once upon a time, there was a weak monkey who wanted to be powerful. He went to the queen and asked, "How do I become powerful, brave and strong?"
"You have to get a key and unlock the magic stone," said the queen.
So he began his journey. He was jumping over logs and climbing up trees. He was having so much fun.
On the way, he met an owl who taught him karate so he could beat the guards who protected the key. He beat the guards and got the key. Then they ran as fast as they could to the stone. Then they got the stone and became the best superheroes in the world.

Poppy (7)
Our Lady Of Lourdes Catholic Primary School, Birkdale

Payton's Zoo Adventure

...at the zoo.

Ellie and Robin the elf went on an adventure. Robin walked Ellie through the entrance. Robin and Ellie went to see the animals. Ellie wanted to ride an elephant with Robin.

Next, Ellie and Robin went to see the panda family. Robin hugged the baby panda and Ellie hugged the big panda.

When Ellie and Robin left the panda family, the elephant flipped them onto his back with his trunk. The elephant stopped beside a monkey who was giving away bananas. Ellie and Robin said thank you to the monkey.

Then Ellie got dropped off at home by Robin and the elephant.

Payton Winning (7)

Our Lady Of Lourdes Catholic Primary School, Birkdale

Milo's Pirate Adventure

...in the sea.

Ellie and Robin were on an old boat on their way to find treasure. They spotted a treasure chest shining in the sun, and in that chest, there were gold coins. They felt happy and excited.

All of a sudden, there was an angry pirate. He had a big sword and he took their treasure.

The pirate made Robin walk the plank and he was very scared of falling into the big sea.

When he jumped into the sea, he landed on a playful dolphin. Ellie wanted to go too, so she also jumped off the plank. They'd had a very exciting adventure but it was time to go home.

Milo Booth (6)

Our Lady Of Lourdes Catholic Primary School, Birkdale

Robyn's Jungle Adventure

...in a jungle in a magical world.

Suddenly, Tinker Bell appeared.

"It is not safe here, come with me," she said, "I will take you to my house."

Ellie arrived at Tinker Bell's house.

"Wow!" Ellie said. "This is amazing!"

The house had a flower on it. It shone in the moonlight. They had some tea and cupcakes while they chatted. After, they danced.

Robin could see that Ellie was tired.

He said, "I think that it is time to go home."

Then Robin took her home and laid her back in her own bed.

Robyn Bradley (7)

Our Lady Of Lourdes Catholic Primary School, Birkdale

Jacob's Adventure

...on a magical island in the deep blue sea. The ocean was filled with tropical fish. The colours were amazing. Ellie felt like she was in a dream.

All of a sudden, a beautiful mermaid swam past. She had light pink hair and her tail looked like a rainbow.

When Ellie landed on the island, a sand monster appeared. He was gigantic. Ellie was terrified.

As the monster approached Ellie, she could see his face looked kind and friendly. He looked happy to see her. They spent loads of time together exploring the island. Ellie didn't want to go home!

Jacob Givin (7)
Our Lady Of Lourdes Catholic Primary School, Birkdale

Jessa's Magical Adventure

...in a magical land.

Robin the elf called a unicorn with his magic and Robin and Ellie climbed on it. Suddenly, the unicorn turned into a dragon. They were shocked.

The dragon started to run after them. They were so scared, they ran away.

The dragon became sad when he saw both of them running away from him, so it turned into a unicorn again. They climbed on the unicorn again and patted his back with love. Suddenly, the unicorn turned into a witch. The witch gifted them a magic broom. They flew safely back to their house on the broom.

Jessa Rose Shinto (7)

Our Lady Of Lourdes Catholic Primary School, Birkdale

Emmy's Magical Adventure

Once upon a time, Ben and Lilly were happily playing on a magical unicorn in the sunny meadows. In the sunny meadows were beautiful bluebells. They were so happy...

Until the unicorn got lost and a dragon came and scared them away. They ran as fast as they could, but the dragon was getting closer...

Luckily, the magical unicorn swooped in and saved Ben and Lilly. They started heading back home.

However, they bumped into a witch but the witch was kind. She gave them a broomstick and they lived happily ever after.

Emmy Duckworth (7)

Our Lady Of Lourdes Catholic Primary School, Birkdale

Max's Space Adventure

...in space. Ellie and the elf flew into space looking at the yellow stars.

Whilst Ellie and the elf were looking at the stars and planets, a sneaky alien was creeping up on them.

Ellie got sucked up by the alien with her teddy.

Ellie and the alien were looking up at the stars.

The alien, Ellie and the elf looked at the creepy monster wiggling its long tongue at them.

The alien and the elf dropped Ellie off at home. She was so happy that she got a ride in a spaceship.

Max Buttworth (7)

Our Lady Of Lourdes Catholic Primary School, Birkdale

Kai's Adventure

There was a new boy in class and his name was Henry.

At break time, Henry made friends with somebody called George. They played hide-and-seek. Henry hid behind a tree and got found pretty soon.

After break time came science. The children studied how oxygen still got into the water.

Next was maths. They learnt what 'times' means.

Then for English, they just copied a story.

At last, it was hometime. Henry got his stuff and said goodbye to his friend and left.

Kai Davidson (7)

Our Lady Of Lourdes Catholic Primary School, Birkdale

Ave Maria's Space Adventure

...up in space.

They heard weird noises but they just ignored them. It was an alien! But the alien was scared and just stared. The alien decided to get in his floating spaceship and when his light came on, they were in the air! They became the best of friends but suddenly they heard a big bang noise. It was a monster! The monster tried to eat them. He put his tongue out and they hid. Eventually, he left.

Then they said bye and went home.

What happened next?

Ave Maria

Our Lady Of Lourdes Catholic Primary School, Birkdale

Emily's Zoo Adventure

...at the entrance gate of the zoo.

They saw a nice giraffe and a smiley elephant.

They jumped onto the elephant's back. Ellie was happy. They met a panda. They hugged the cosy panda. The panda was nice and soft.

They got back on the elephant and walked through the jungle until they saw a monkey! Ellie and Robin saw the monkey and said hi. They became friends and they had bananas. Then Robin sent Ellie home and then Ellie went to sleep again.

Emily Kate Hammond (7)

Our Lady Of Lourdes Catholic Primary School, Birkdale

Jotham's Space Adventure

...in space.

They stood on the moon and gazed up at the stars.

Suddenly, Ellie began to float. She was surprised. Then she saw a little teddy. Then she met a crew of aliens. She made friends and played with them and had fun.

After that, they saw a monster underneath them. They were scared, very worried and anxious.

Finally, they arrived home. She had had an amazing adventure. She was happy and said bye to her friends.

Jotham Oyedokun (7)

Our Lady Of Lourdes Catholic Primary School, Birkdale

Sophie's Adventure

Once upon a time, there was a little gymnast called Chloe. Chloe loved gymnastics. It was her passion.

One day at regionals, she slipped and she failed for the first time. That evening, she cried all night.

All she did was practise for the next week.

The next time she had a competition, she came in first place.

One day, she failed again. But that time, she knew... All she needed to do was practise!

Sophie Monk (7)

Our Lady Of Lourdes Catholic Primary School, Birkdale

Eva's Zoo Adventure

...at the zoo.

They found an elephant. They had a ride on the elephant around the zoo. Then they met a panda with a baby panda. They were so happy.

The elephant took them to see some other animals and they saw a monkey. The monkey gave them a banana. They went home when it was night-time. They'd had a great time.

Eva Serban (7)

Our Lady Of Lourdes Catholic Primary School, Birkdale

Luke's Space Adventure

...into outer space. They were on the way to the moon.

Soon they arrived at the moon and started picking stars.

Then an alien sucked up the girl.

The alien wanted to be friends.

They saw one of the alien's friends, who wanted to play.

They said goodbye to the aliens when they dropped her off.

Luke Latham (7)

Our Lady Of Lourdes Catholic Primary School, Birkdale

Vincent's Space Adventure

...in space.

Robin pulled Ellie out into the cold night sky. The shiny gold stars twinkled as the sky darkened. Robin and Ellie landed on a strange moon-shaped planet. There was an alien who usually wore the stars as earrings. They became friends.

Vincent Witter (7)

Our Lady Of Lourdes Catholic Primary School, Birkdale

Reggie's Space Adventure

...in outer space.

They landed on the moon and saw sparkly stars.

Then they found an alien who was laughing as he had never seen humans before.

Reggie Hindle (6)

Our Lady Of Lourdes Catholic Primary School, Birkdale

Hannah's First Story

Once upon a time, there was a playful unicorn and she was lovely and cute. She was helping some cute children, it was a boy and a girl. The girl was little.

Suddenly, a red dragon came. He was scary and the children were frightened so they ran away as fast as they could. As they were running, the little girl said, "Argh!" and the little boy said, "Don't worry," as they saw the magical unicorn.

So they got onto the helpful unicorn and the pretty unicorn was running. The children said, "Yay!" as they were happy.

Then they met a wicked witch, but she was helpful and gave them her brown, old, special broomstick.

Finally, they got on the brown, old and special broomstick and the children said, "Yay, wow!"

Hannah Natsai Jaratina (6)

The Wickford CE School, Wickford

Ralphie's Pirate Adventure

One day, Ellie and Jack were on a wooden, brown boat. The big yellow sun was shining and their teddy bear was smiling.

They eventually arrived at a Caribbean island and the bear was impressed. But they were wary of a greedy, clever pirate.

"Avast me hearties!" said the pirate.

Ellie was scared, the bear said, "I am too." Jack was brave and fought the pirate.

The pirate forced Ellie and Jack to walk the plank, so they did.

They were having fun. Suddenly, the bear fell into the water. Ellie was upset. Jack jumped into the water to get the bear.

Eventually, pirates Jack and Ellie arrived at home sweet home, at least for them it was.

Ralphie W (6)

The Wickford CE School, Wickford

Valerie's First Story

One beautiful day, the elf Robin and Ellie arrived at a big land, it was so pretty. "Hooray!" But they had landed in the dragons' land. "Oh no!" said the children. They ran off and so did their teddy bear. "Argh!" A unicorn saved the children. "Yay! We love you, Unicorn!" said the children. Then they flew to a witch's land, but the witch was kind.
"Take my broom!"
"Yay!" said the children.
"Thank you," said Robin and Ellie.

Valerie Pinkovska (6)
The Wickford CE School, Wickford

Luca's Pirate Adventure

Once upon a time, there was a boy and a girl on a boat. They were happy together until the boy saw a pirate ship heading towards them.

"Shiver me sails, kids get on my ship!" said the pirate.

"Argh!" said the kids.

"Walk the plank," said the pirate.

So they did. They were scared.

Soon they went on some dolphins' backs and went to the shore.

They had had enough and went home.

Luca Jones (6)
The Wickford CE School, Wickford

Calla's Jungle Adventure

Once upon a time, there lived a little girl called Ellie and a boy called Robin. They went to the jungle. They swung on the vines. They saw a snake, he was fierce. He chased Ellie and Robin. "Hiss!" said the snake.
They saw a lion, he was cute. The lion let Ellie ride him home.
They swung on the vines home.

Calla (6)

The Wickford CE School, Wickford

Prarthana's First Story

One beautiful day, there was a beautiful unicorn and a girl and boy. The girl and boy found a scary dragon. "Argh!" said the girl and boy. The girl and boy ran and ran to the unicorn. They found the unicorn. The girl and boy found a home, the home had a witch.
The girl and boy went home.

Prarthana Sreedevi (5)
The Wickford CE School, Wickford

Jude's Pirate Adventure

One day some children were sailing on a sunny day.

They got to an island and they found treasure.

They met a pirate.

The pirate forced them to walk the plank, they were scared.

They rode on some friendly dolphins.

They finally got home.

Jude Vince (6)

The Wickford CE School, Wickford

Poppy's Space Adventure

...in space!

"Do you know what that is?" he asked.

"It's a flying saucer!" she said.

They went in it.

They saw an alien called Mr Alien.

Finally, Ellie was back home.

Poppy Crittenden (6)

The Wickford CE School, Wickford

Sofia-Belle's Zoo Adventure

Ellie and Robin went to the lovely zoo. Ellie and Robin rode an elephant. They saw a fluffy panda. They rode the elephant again. They ate a yummy banana. They said goodbye.

Sofia-Belle (6)

The Wickford CE School, Wickford

Kathleen's Magical Adventure

One day a little boy and girl were riding on a unicorn. A dragon scared the little girl and boy away. The unicorn took them away. A witch came to see them.

Kathleen Johnson (6)

The Wickford CE School, Wickford

Forrest's Jungle Adventure

Soon they arrived at the jungle... but then they were so excited that they didn't notice that the vines would snap...

Snap! The vines snapped. They even landed on a snake's body. The snake looked puzzled and this is what he said in a deep voice: "Buzz off you two!" But it did not see Ted the bear. They didn't want to see that snake again so they ran to some leaves.

"Surprise!" said a lion. "The name is Jake," said the lion in a deep voice. "Do you want a ride, you three?"

"Yes!"

"Woo hoo!" said Ted. "This is fun."

"Not fun, fabulous!" said Ellie. "This reminds me of some other people in the old days."

"Here we are," said the lion.

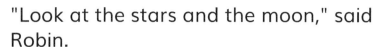

"Look at the stars and the moon," said Robin.
"Yes, this is my dirt path."

Forrest Harris (6)
Thorns Primary School, Quarry Bank

Mason's Jungle Adventure

...at the jungle. They loved the jungle! They swung on the vines and a cute bear followed them and they carried on.

Soon they met a snake. "Hello," they said. The snake replied, "Hello. Looks like you are in a rush."

"We are. Do you want to come with us?"

"Yes."

"Run!" The snake was chasing them.

"Phew, I did not like that. Let's carry on."

They met a tiger. "Do you want a ride?"

"Yes okay."

"Come on, hop on my back."

"Whee! We loved that, can we do that again?"

"Yes you can, maybe later."

They swung home and walked home and they went home and they lived happily ever after.

Mason Jones (6)

Thorns Primary School, Quarry Bank

Nevaeh's Jungle Adventure

Soon they arrived at the jungle. They were swinging around. It was really fun swinging around. They kept going.

"Oh no, a snake, run! We have got to go the other way."

"But how?" said Ellie.

"Let's just go the other way. Run!"

"What do we do now?"

"We have to just leave now. Run as fast as you can!"

A tiger was under the leaves. "This is bad."

"Shh."

He was smiling. "I won't eat you."

"We thank you, tiger. I love that he helped us run away, I didn't think he would do that."

They went back home and it was time for bed. It was really fun there.

Nevaeh Higginson (5)

Thorns Primary School, Quarry Bank

Percy's Jungle Adventure

They whooshed on the vines and they had fun. It was spiky but they were having too much fun so they did not notice.

Then they noticed there was a really long snake. They were worried but then it ran after them. "Run, run!"

Ellie and Robin ran as fast as they could go. Then suddenly they lost the snake.

Then they met a lion. The cute teddy was extremely scared but then it bent and they hopped on and it was fun, very fun. The jungle was beautiful. After riding the lion they finally got home.

"It was fun but now I need to have a good night's sleep at home."

Percy Jackson (6)
Thorns Primary School, Quarry Bank

Bobby's Jungle Adventure

Ellie and Robin arrived at the jungle. They were swinging and it was fun! They saw a teddy swinging and the teddy was laughing. They saw a snake, its name was Percy. Robin said, "It's a snake!" Ellie was scared. They ran away with the teddy and they never saw the snake again.

They saw a lion named Harry. Robin and Ellie were scared. The teddy was holding Ellie's hand. The teddy was scared. The lion was friendly and let Ellie, Robin and Teddy ride on his back. They had fun. The teddy was on the lion's head. They didn't want the day to end.

Bobby Simpson (6)

Thorns Primary School, Quarry Bank

Ryan's Jungle Adventure

They arrived at the jungle. Robin said, "This is fun," as they were swinging on their vines. They saw a snake and ran. Robin and Ellie were scared. "Come on, run, it might eat us!" But after ten minutes the snake got lost.

Then they met a lion and he looked at them suspiciously. Ellie said, "Can we have a ride home?"

"Yes you can, just give me whatever is in your pockets. No, just kidding, it's free today. Hop on."

They got home. Their mom wondered where they were. It was a mystery.

Ryan Sandland (6)
Thorns Primary School, Quarry Bank

Willow's Jungle Adventure

Ellie and Robin the elf were in the jungle. Ellie loved the swing, so did Robin the elf. Ellie and Robin the elf saw the snake and its name was Slither. The snake was big and it had a big tongue. Slither the snake was following Ellie and Robin the elf so they ran away.

When Ellie and Robin the elf ran away they saw a lion. "Hop on my back, I will give you a ride," said the lion.

Swing swing! "I see my house, let's go on the bars."

"Okay," said Robin the elf.

Willow Dunn (6)
Thorns Primary School, Quarry Bank

Daisy's Jungle Adventure

Ellie and Robin the elf were swinging on big branches. They were having lots of fun.
They saw a friendly snake called Sliders.
Ellie thought he would hurt them but...
Sliders was friendly. They ran away from the snake because he was not friendly! They were crying with tears.
Then they met a lion who was friendly. Ellie thought the lion was mean but he was friendly.
Roary took them home like a friendly lion. They were laughing. They were swinging on the branches.

Daisy Hadlington-Jones (6)
Thorns Primary School, Quarry Bank

Georgia's Jungle Adventure

Ellie and Robin were at the jungle. They climbed on the swings and they loved the swings. But then they saw a snake and they didn't know how to go over the snake.

The snake was chasing Ellie and Robin but they were running as fast as they could.

They saw a tiger and Ellie and Robin were scared, they didn't know what to do. But the tiger was being kind so Ellie and Robin went on the tiger.

Then finally they were at home swinging on the swings.

Georgia John (6)

Thorns Primary School, Quarry Bank

Freya's Jungle Adventure

One night Ellie heard a tap on her window. It was Robin. He said, "Would you like to go to the jungle?"

They went to see a snake and Ellie was afraid and Robin protected her from the snake. They ran away from the snake as fast as they could. It was so scary.

They made friends with a lion and it was cute and beautiful.

They went on the lion home and went out of sight. Then they went back to their houses on the vines.

Freya Hope (5)

Thorns Primary School, Quarry Bank

Jorgie's Jungle Adventure

Ellie and Robin arrived at the jungle. They were swinging and it was fun! They saw a teddy. The teddy was climbing up the branch.

They saw a snake. They were scared of the snake. The snake was called Bobby. They ran away from the snake. Robin was looking at the snake and the teddy was looking at the snake.

They saw a lion named Forrest. They had a ride on the lion. The lion was looking at Ellie and Robin.

They went home.

Jorgie Cutler (6)

Thorns Primary School, Quarry Bank

Daniel's Jungle Adventure

Ellie and Robin arrived at the jungle vines and some were big or small.
Next they met a snake in the jungle and they were afraid of him. They ran away.
Next they hid. The cat found them. They found a lion and they weren't afraid of him. They got on him. Ellie and Robin and the bear ran away on the lion.
Next they went home from the jungle and they were best friends forever.

Daniel Berg (6)

Thorns Primary School, Quarry Bank

Aurora's Adventure

...at a school! They were looking at this school, it was amazing.

They played hopscotch, it was great. Then they got to a playground. It had lots of people. They went in a cart to a farm. The farmer said they could keep a cow!

Aurora Sangha (5)

Thorns Primary School, Quarry Bank

Sofia's Jungle Adventure

At the jungle Ellie and Robin were swinging. They met a snake. They ran away from the snake.
They met a lion. They had a ride on the lion. Then they went home.

Sofia Burgess (6)

Thorns Primary School, Quarry Bank

Noah's Jungle Adventure

Ellie and Robin went to the jungle. They saw a snake. They ran away from the snake. They hid from the snake.
They ran away with a lion. They went home.

Noah Prosser (6)
Thorns Primary School, Quarry Bank

Darcie-May's Jungle Adventure

... at the jungle. Ellie, the seven-year-old, swung from vine to vine with her rainbow teddy. They went through the trees and leaves. They went a very, very long way through the jungle.

Finally, they reached a tree but they didn't realise that there was a talking, angry and fierce snake. It was scary. It was big. It was stripy. The snake was tired. Ellie woke him up.

Ellie and Robin had to run as fast as they could. They got to the end of the trees. They had to jump but the snake got down off the tree. Ellie and Robin had to run again.

They met a lion. Ellie was worried but they realised it was a friendly lion. Ellie thought lions were meant to be nasty and mean. The lion said, "Hop on my back!"

So they got a ride. It was very fast. They reached the end of the jungle.

Ellie said, "Beware of the snake!"
Ellie and Robin went back home.
Ellie said, "That was a fun adventure!" with a yawn.
Robin said, "Yes, it was a fun adventure, wasn't it?"

Darcie-May Weldon (7)

West Pelton Primary School, Stanley

Ben's Jungle Adventure

...in the deep dark jungle. Ellie and Robin met a bear. He was a talking, cuddly bear. Next, Ellie and the elf were greeted by a big hissing python. The sneaky snake wanted to eat them up.

Then it tried to eat them but they ran too quickly for the snake. Then Robin spotted a hiding spot. Ellie and Robin jumped in a hole.

After Ellie and Robin jumped down from the tree. A bush started to move. Robin looked in the bush. There was a lion. The lion was ginormous.

Then the giant lion let Ellie and Robin jump on his back. The lion pounced out of the bush and ran. It was fun. Then the lion let Ellie and Robin off.

Finally, they asked the lion how to get home. Then they made it home.

Ben Robson (7)
West Pelton Primary School, Stanley

Ellie's Space Adventure

...in space. Ellie and Robin landed on the silvery moon. They collected a pocket full of shiny sparkly stars.

When they landed, Benji the white ghost-like alien wanted to steal them.

Benji jumped into his spaceship made of metal and jewels. He zapped up Ellie and her teddy, called Sparkle.

Robin was zapped into Benji's friend, Alijy's spaceship. They quickly followed and somersaulted through the dark night.

Ellie and Robin and the aliens were in the metal spaceship.

The alien and Robin took Ellie home. They said goodbye and her teddy bear said goodbye as well.

Ellie Ramsey (6)

West Pelton Primary School, Stanley

Aliya's Pirate Adventure

...on the sea. The elf took Ellie to a sunny and bright island.

The boat landed on the island and they found treasure.

The elf said, "Get down because you might hurt yourself."

A pirate came to the island. They didn't know what he was.

"Do you want to go to my ship?"

"Yes, we would like to go to your ship."

Then they jumped on the dolphin and the dolphin took them home.

They walked home.

Aliya Docherty (6)

West Pelton Primary School, Stanley

Ayla's Space Adventure

...in space. Robin and Ellie flew through the fluffy clouds.

Kai was looking for a machine because he wanted new people to come to his planet.

Ellie was going into the spaceship. She let the teddy go first.

They flew in the sky. There was another spaceship behind them.

Another alien was trying to eat the spaceship but he couldn't but he tried and tried again.

Then they said goodbye to Ellie and they went off.

Ayla Tiffen (6)

West Pelton Primary School, Stanley

Scarlett's Magical Adventure

...in a magical land. Ellie and the elf went on a trip to the woods with a unicorn.
The dragon blew fire at Ellie and the elf.
Ellie and the elf ran away from the dragon so that they didn't get set on fire.
Ellie and the elf rode on the magic unicorn. They flew in the sky.
The witch gave the children sweets.
They went on the broomstick back home.

Scarlett Pears (6)

West Pelton Primary School, Stanley

Archie's Magical Adventure

...in a magical land. The beautiful unicorn took them on a trip.

A dragon appeared. The dragon flew higher than them.

The dragon was breathing fire and they ran away because they were scared.

They went on the magic unicorn and flew into the sky.

When they landed they met a witch who had sweets.

The witch gave them a broomstick to ride home.

Archie Brannen (5)

West Pelton Primary School, Stanley

Shay's Jungle Adventure

...in a jungle. Ellie and Robin flew through the sky.

Ellie and Robin met a long snake who was strange.

The long, windy snake was scaring the children and they ran away.

A friendly lion came and rescued the children.

They rode the lion to a safe place.

They decided to live in the jungle because it was great.

Shay Thomas (6)

West Pelton Primary School, Stanley

Ruby's Pirate Adventure

...on the sea. They were rowing to a desert island.

When they got to the desert island they saw treasure.

A pirate came and caught Ellie and the elf with the treasure.

They got trapped on the pirate ship and they were frightened.

They had fun riding on the dolphins.

They had a fun adventure.

Ruby Brown (6)

West Pelton Primary School, Stanley

Terry's Pirate Adventure

...on the sea. Robin and Ellie arrived by their wooden boat at a mystery island.
When they landed on the golden sand, they were amazed to see a golden treasure chest.
A pirate appeared. They showed him the treasure.
The pirate took them onto his ship.

Terry Joe Oakes (6)
West Pelton Primary School, Stanley

Joe's Magical Adventure

...in a magical land. They have gone to the forest to climb some trees with the unicorn. The scary dragon scared the children with his fire.
They ran away.
The magical unicorn came and saved them.
They were so happy.

Joe Brown (6)

West Pelton Primary School, Stanley

Joe's Zoo Adventure

...in a zoo. They went into the zoo.
The elephant was in the zoo.
They went to feed the panda.
They rode on the back of the elephant.

Joe Addison (5)
West Pelton Primary School, Stanley

The Storyboards

Here are the fun storyboards
children could choose from...

MAGICAL ADVENTURE

JUNGLE TALE

PIRATE ADVENTURE

SPACE STORY

ZOO ADVENTURE

Young Writers Information

We hope you have enjoyed reading this book and that you will continue to in the coming years.

If you're a young writer who enjoys reading and creative writing, or the parent of an enthusiastic poet or story writer, do visit our website **www.youngwriters.co.uk**. Here you will find free competitions, workshops and games, as well as recommended reads, a poetry glossary and our blog.

If you would like to order further copies of this book, or any of our other titles give us a call or visit **www.youngwriters.co.uk**.

Young Writers
Remus House
Coltsfoot Drive
Peterborough
PE2 9BF

(01733) 890066
info@youngwriters.co.uk

Scan to watch the
My First Story video!

f YoungWritersUK   🐦 YoungWritersCW

📷 youngwriterscw   ♪ youngwriterscw